Rockets

HAUNTED MOUSE

Magenta and the
Ghost Bride

Dee Shulman

A & C Black • London

Rockets series:

CROOK CATCHERS - Karen Wallace & Judy Brown

HAUNTED MOUSE - Dee Shulman

LITTLE T - Frank Rodgers

MOTLEY'S CREW - Margaret Ryan & Margaret Chamberlain

MR CROC - Frank Rodgers

MRS MAGIC - Wendy Smith

MY FUNNY FAMILY - Colin West

ROVER - Chris Powling & Scoular Anderson

SILLY SAUSAGE - Michaela Morgan & Dee Shulman

WIZARD'S BOY - Scoular Anderson

First paperback edition 2002
First published 2002 in hardback by A & C Black (Publishers) Ltd
37 Soho Square, London W1D 3QZ

Text and illustrations copyright © 2002 Dee Shulman

The right of Dee Shulman to be identified as author
and illustrator of this work has been asserted by her
in accordance with the Copyright, Designs and Patents Act 1988.

ISBN 0-7136-5975-0

A CIP catalogue record for this book is available
from the British Library.

Printed and bound by G. Z. Printek, Bilbao, Spain.

Chapter One

HOWLLLL HOWLLL HOWLLL

It was a lovely sunny morning, but Magenta the Haunted Mouse didn't feel very bright.

HOWLLLLL HOWLL

YAWN!

No one in the Haunted House had been getting any peace.

Oliver tried to look wise.

Ridley stroked his whiskers.

Hmm...

The other ghosts blinked blankly...

...including Loretta, who was usually quite helpful.

Poor Sir Boris. I can't think what's wrong!

HOWLL

HOWLL

HOWLL

Magenta sighed.

So Magenta climbed the stairs very slowly indeed.

Chapter Two

Magenta tapped on Sir Boris's door – very quietly.

VISITORS NOT WELCOME

HOWLLLL

Er... Maybe I'll come back later!

She was just scampering away when Sir Boris appeared in front of her.

S-S-Sir Boris!

Did you want something, Small Mouse?

Magenta followed Sir Boris back into his room. But before she could open her mouth to speak, he started wailing again.

HOWLLL HOWLLL

She covered her ears and waited...

HOWLLLLLL

...and waited...

Yawn

HOWLLL HOWLLL

...and waited...

HOWLLLLLL

Magenta's doing well up there!

She certainly knows how to handle Sir Boris. Tee Hee!

8

At last Sir Boris had to stop howling to yawn, and Magenta spoke.

'What?' squeaked Magenta.

'Well, all the animals are jumping around with their wives and families having fun... even that rotten rat Ridley has got a girlfriend... it just... isn't fair!'

'Do you mean... are you trying to say... that you want a... *girlfriend*?' asked Magenta.

Magenta looked puzzled.

And he started howling louder than ever. Magenta crept quietly away.

Chapter Three

Magenta called a meeting.

13

The animals had lots of ideas.

'How could anyone find a wife good enough for Sir Boris?' muttered Loretta in a quiet voice, as everyone filed out of the room.

But nobody heard.

Magenta turned to Oliver, who puffed up his feathers, importantly.

'Have you learnt anything about a *ghost bride* Oliver?' interrupted Magenta impatiently.

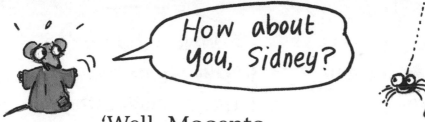

'Well, Magenta,
I did a fair bit of spying
and I did see three ghosts –
one quite hopeful as a bride...'

'...until *she* turned round!'

Ridley leaned forward. 'Over the hill, across the river, on the other side of the deep, dark wood there's a spooky castle...'

'...where a bootiful ghost lives called The Lady Bella Donna.'

And from what I hear, she is on the lookout for a new husband.

'What happened to the old husband?' asked Loretta quietly, but nobody heard.

'Ridley – you're brilliant!' beamed Magenta.

'Oliver, could you fly *me* to the big spooky castle where the bootiful Lady Bella Donna lives?'

Well– I don't see why not!

'Hooray!' cried Magenta.

A wife for Sir Boris! Now he'll stop howling, and we can all get some peace!

Only Loretta didn't dance.

Poor Sir Boris!

23

Chapter Five

Oliver and Magenta set off, while all the other animals started preparing for the most wonderful wedding party.

The spiders began spinning a long, lacy veil.

That's **so** pretty!

Aren't they clever!

The mice started gathering piles of tasty snacks...

The rats got busy brewing a basinful of bubbling bog-beer...

And the ghosts began working on some wedding music...

27

Chapter Six

Loretta was still crying when the sound of ghostly hooves came clattering up the hill.

All the animals gathered round to welcome The Lady Bella Donna. But she wasn't quite what they had expected.

Then she looked up at the Haunted House.

'And what about the stable for my darling Dazzle?'

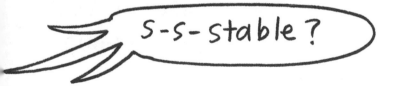

S-s-stable?

Slowly, The Lady Bella Donna made her way into the house. The animals and ghosts followed mournfully behind her.

Her mood didn't improve inside the Haunted House.

'Would you horrible lot stop snuffling down my neck and clean up this disgusting mess. What is that gross pile of rags doing there?'

Our lovely veil!

Our delicious banquet!

'And somebody glide along and fill me a nice, steamy bath...'

... You-girl, off you go!

-b-but...

'The rest of you can tell Sir Boris I will be ready to marry him in two hours precisely.'

And The Lady Bella Donna wafted off.

The animals were horrified.

35

Chapter Seven

'Ahem... Sir Boris...'

What is it Mouse?

We've found you a bride, but...

Sir Boris beamed.

You **have?** Well that's jolly fine. Where is she?

'She's having a bath but...'

But **what?**

'Well she's... she's...'
Magenta tried to tell him.

She's not **old** and **ugly** is she?

'No she's... pretty... but...'

'Well – um yes – but...' stuttered Magenta.

'Well off you go then, Mouse – I have to get ready!' said Sir Boris.

'The mouse tells me Sir Boris is very handsome...' said The Lady Bella Donna.

'Well I need at least twenty...' she added.

'Oh no! There are no servants here...' cried Loretta.

Chapter Eight

The animals all gathered in the great hall for the ceremony.

Sir Boris waited impatiently for his bride.

The hour struck, and The Lady Bella
Donna wafted in.

And knelt beside Sir Boris.

Eager to greet his bride, Sir Boris stood up, as The Lady Bella Donna turned for the first time to face him.

'Hey, magnificent catch Loretta,' said Sir Boris admiringly.

She turned towards him.

He looked at her and gasped.

'Oh Sir Boris – I've waited a hundred years for you to ask!'

'I think there will be a wedding after all!' squeaked Magenta happily.

Chapter Nine

The newlyweds were so happy that they sang of their love all night long.